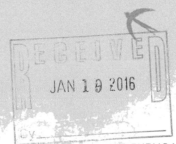

BIG FRIENDS

Henry Holt and Company, LLC • *Publishers since 1866*
175 Fifth Avenue, New York, New York 10010 • mackids.com

Henry Holt® is a registered trademark of Henry Holt and Company, LLC.
Text copyright © 2014 by Linda Sarah • Illustrations copyright © 2014 by Benji Davies • All rights reserved.
First published in the United States in 2016 by Henry Holt and Company, LLC. • Originally published in Great Britain in 2014 by Simon & Schuster UK Ltd.

Library of Congress Cataloging-in-Publication Data
Sarah, Linda, author.
[On Sudden Hill]
Big friends / Linda Sarah ; Benji Davies. — First American edition.
pages cm
First published: London : Simon & Schuster Childrens Books, 2014 under the title On Sudden Hill.
Summary: Best friends Etho and Birt love going up Sudden Hill and sitting in simple cardboard boxes imagining they are kings,
soldiers, astronauts, or pirates until Shu asks to join them, and their "two-by-two rhythm" is disturbed.
ISBN 978-1-62779-330-8 (hardcover)
[1. Best friends—Fiction. 2. Friendship—Fiction. 3. Imagination—Fiction. 4. Play—Fiction.] I. Davies, Benji, illustrator. II. Title.
PZ7.S2393Big 2016   [E]—dc23   2015005998

Henry Holt books may be purchased for business or promotional use. For information on bulk purchases, please contact the Macmillan
Corporate and Premium Sales Department at (800) 221-7945 x5442 or by e-mail at specialmarkets@macmillan.com.
First American Edition—2016 • Printed in China by Toppan Leefung Printing, Ltd.,
Dongguan City, Guangdong Province

1 2 3 4 5 6 7 8 9 10

For Stephen
—L. S.

For Auntie Jan
and summers spent
painting at Pondok
—B. D.

BIG FRIENDS

Linda Sarah & Benji Davies

HENRY HOLT AND COMPANY
NEW YORK

Two cardboard boxes,
big enough to sit in, hide inside.

Birt and Etho take them out each day,
climb up Sudden Hill, and sit in them.

Sometimes they're kings,
soldiers, astronauts.
Sometimes they're pirates
sailing wild seas and skies.

But always, always,
they're Big friends.

Their sailing, running, leaping, flying,
their chatter and giggles,
him and Etho,

their silences
and watching small movements
in the valley and feeling
big as Giant Kings.

Birt loves their two-by-two rhythm.

And then one Monday
(it's cramping cold)
they meet another box-carrier,
who wants to join them.

This tiny boy's called Shu.
He's watched Birt and Etho every day
and finally found a big enough box
and courage to ask if he can play, too.

Etho smiles and says, "Sure!"
And so the three sit in their boxes,
watch one kestrel
and two lost clouds.

Sometimes they're dragon slayers,
side-by-side house dwellers,
and skyscraper dancers.

But Birt feels strange.

One night,
Birt smashes his box,
stamps on it,
rips it to bits.

His dad shouts something flat from the front room
about being quiet and that's enough!

Birt stops going up Sudden Hill.

Etho and Shu
stop by sometimes.
Birt avoids them.

Instead he stays at home,
mostly drawing pictures
of two boxes, side by side.

But he misses Etho.
He misses their cardboard
castles on Sudden Hill.

One day,
a knock on the door.

He hears Shu's voice.
"We made you something.
Please come out!"

All Birt can see
as he peeks
from the curtain
is a box.

But it's much,
much more
than a box.

It's got bright, waving things
attached to it like huge kites.
It's got colors.
It's got sound.
It's got, it's got—WHEELS!

The HUGE box-on-wheels
(that they call Mr. ClimbFierce)
is hauled up Sudden Hill.

It's amazing!

An incredible Monster-Creature-Box Thing!

It's a supersonic rocket blaster!
A triple jet transformer!
A sparkling glitter king!

It's even got boxes inside,
one with cookies, one with lemonade.

Birt likes Shu.

Shu is kind.

Shu is funny.

Shu is daring and brave.

Birt loves their time together,
their Etho-Shu-Birt-iness.

He loves their three-by-three rhythm.

It's new.

And it's good.